The Maid of Artemis

OLIVIA COOLIDGE

Illustrated by Bea Holmes

1969

HOUGHTON MIFFLIN COMPANY BOSTON

Other Books by OLIVIA COOLIDGE

Greek Myths
Legends of the North
The Trojan War
Egyptian Adventures
Cromwell's Head
Roman People
Winston Churchill
and the Story of Two World Wars
Caesar's Gallic War
Men of Athens
Makers of the Red Revolution
People in Palestine
Lives of Famous Romans
The King of Men
Marathon Looks on the Sea
George Bernard Shaw

Contents

Introduction

MEN HAVE EXCAVATED the temple of Artemis at Brauron, and when I went there a few years ago, they were doing so still. They have lifted some of the fallen columns and put them back in place; and they can show you the frames of the beds, just big enough for children. The statues they have found are in the museum at Athens, the little girl with the rabbit and other little girls, given by their fathers in memory of their service in the temple.

Up in the long shed, where bits and pieces are laid out in hopes of finding some which belong together, lay a small marble hand holding a bird, carefully and tenderly so as not to hurt it. From its fine workmanship, we can guess at the beauty of the statue which has vanished.

I wondered at that hand because the artist has expressed the tenderness of the little girl, in spite of the fact that the bird was her sacrifice at the altar of Artemis. Next I began to think about how quickly girls had to grow up in those days, how much life demanded of women, how little could be done to help mothers bear their children or rear them until they were grown. In spite of this, we cannot suppose Greek women were unhappy, or that the stages of their growing were not as natural to them as ours are to us.

In this way a story developed, but the archaeologist who finds one hand holding a bird lays it aside until he discovers the whole statue. If he does not, he simply puts up with what he has. The storyteller must patch the old things together with stuff of his own. There was a bear dance of some sort, but we hardly know what. The legend of Iphigenia has come down to us, but the rites of Artemis are long forgotten and can only be guessed from a few hints. We cannot know the appearance of the image and can only imagine that it was not originally Greek. But we do know little girls and can think what growing meant to them inside their own world, so different from ours. If Ala grew up fitted for the life she was going to lead, then she was happy; and her parents in their way had been wise for her.

The
Maid
of
Artemis

———

The
Special
Day

THE HEART OF CONON'S HOUSE was the women's
court, where the loving nature of its mistress Athenais gave it warmth. In the flame of tiny lamps
which the servants had kindled because the sun was
not quite up, the gray-green eyes of Athenais spar-
kled with eagerness for the new day. She turned
to Eunice with a smile; and Eunice, short, sturdy,
and gray haired, smiled back.

"Sandas is helping the boy, Mistress. They will
not be long," Eunice said. "Are you ready, girls?
Phyllis, are you sure that wreath will fit his head?"

Phyllis, who was holding a garland of ivy leaves,
giggled in her stupid way; but Callina, who was
sharp and sly and often needed watching, answered
pertly, "Surely, Eunice, Phyllis's fingers may be
trusted to twist one wreath without your help."

"Oh Callina," said her mistress gently, "do not
spoil our day before it has begun."

Callina lowered her dark eyes, while Eunice

pressed her lips together and looked angry. The silence was awkward; but it was soon broken by Sandas, the boy's attendant, coming into the court.

Sandas was an old man, nearly sixty with white hair and beard. He was tall and thin with stooping shoulders and dressed in a wool robe which fell to his ankles. It was new today and had been bleached to the palest of cream colors, while his girdle, which was of linen, gleamed snow-white.

"How fine you look, Sandas," Athenais greeted him. Sandas beamed.

"Just wait till you see the young master!" He took Cleitos by the hand and drew him into the circle of lamplight to show his new clothes to the women.

Cleitos stood shyly smiling at the fuss that was being made, but pleased about it. He was fifteen years of age, lean, brown, and built like a runner. Dark hair, brushed smooth on the top of his head, had been twisted at the ends into flat curls which lay across his forehead and dipped behind his ears as though they formed a garland. He wore a white woolen tunic exposing bare knees. Its girdle, on which Eunice had spent great pains, was embroidered in blue and gold with touches of scarlet. But the glory of his costume was the cloak.

The old brown cloak which Cleitos wore to school or when he went out with his father was a long and clumsy thing which he had to wrap so tightly about him that he could not swing his arms because young boys were supposed to be modest in public. For the procession today, his mother had woven a short blue cloak which hung freely from his shoulders. Before her marriage, Athenais had been one of the maidens who worked yearlong to weave a new robe for the goddess Athene. In that year, the garment had been more wonderful than ever. Now, therefore, Phyllis said "Ooh!" as she looked at the cloak's border, while Callina cried eagerly, "Even that maiden who challenged the goddess in weaving could not have done better than our mistress!"

"Well said, Callina!"

Callina jumped nervously because the master had come from the men's part of the house and was standing behind her. Praise from Conon was rare because he thought Callina was too free with her tongue. This morning, however, Callina had been lucky because Conon wanted to conceal his pride in his handsome son. He took a fold of the cloak in his hand because he did not think it fit to show pleasure in the cock of his son's head, or his regular features, or the red-brown of his cheek, or his trained muscles. "See how deep the color is!" he said. "Your mother's skill grows greater, so that my cloak is quite outshone."

These were kind words because Conon was dressed for the procession in a gorgeous scarlet cloak with gold threads in the border. He was taking no part in the games, which were only for boys; but he was an Olympic victor and had on his head the crown of wild olive which none but they might wear. No public festival was complete without the men who had brought this honor to Athens.

Athenais smiled happily at her husband. "You must not only look at my gift. Everyone in the household has something for Cleitos on this day. See how beautiful is the pattern on his girdle! Eunice did it, though you know how her eyes pain her over fine work. Phyllis has made the garland, and Callina has a present of her own."

Callina's gift was her most precious thing, a dull red luck-stone which she had strung on a ribbon to lend to Cleitos for the day. This was good of Callina because a luck-stone would sometimes change after being worn by a strange person, so that it no longer had any power for its real owner.

"Sandas was working late last night over something," Athenais said. "I do not know what it was."

Delighted, Sandas brought out from the folds of his tunic a roll of papyrus tied with a bright ribbon which the mistress had given him out of her store. He undid it carefully.

"It is only a poem of Pindar's," he said, "but I have copied it fairly, and it is one that Pindar wrote for a youth who won the footrace in Apollo's games at Delphi." He shook his head. "I fear that Pindar never came to Athens for the games of Theseus or watched our young boys run. Yet I thought this not unfitting for today."

The boy took the poem from Sandas's hand and looked at it. He swallowed silently and ran his tongue around his lips as though they were dry. "I thank you, Sandas . . . thank you . . ." he said in a nervous little voice. "But if . . ."

"I must give my gift, too," cried Conon gaily. "Today I have a second athlete in my family, and I must wish him luck." The gift he presented was only a little oil flask and a scraper, which athletes used to cleanse themselves of dust and sweat. But the scraper was carved ivory, the oil was delicately scented, while the flask itself was a Corinthian masterpiece, white and slender with a single figure outlined on it in fine brown strokes: an athlete binding

the ribbon which was given to victors around his
hair.

The boy looked at the lovely thing, and for the
second time his tongue came out to wet his lips.
They seemed to tremble. "Yes, but . . ." he said,
and stopped to clear his throat. "Yes, but . . . I
may not win."

Athenais caught her breath. So the boy knew
that he was not the fastest runner of his year! Perhaps he had already lost a practice race in the exercise ground. How would his father, who was himself so famous, bear his defeat? She turned sadly
to Conon, who looked in his scarlet and gold like
the god of the sun. But Conon was smiling easily.

"Have you forgotten that when I ran the first
time at the Olympic games, I failed to win? Let me
tell you what my father said when I came to him,
raging against myself and the god who had de-
nied me glory.

" 'My son,' my father said, 'life offers many
chances for glory. If you fail at one, why, you will
find another. Let us talk today of what will matter
more. All year you have trained in dust and heat,
in rain and mud, while your friends were taking
things easy. It is not the winning which makes a
man, but the effort. Let us rejoice in the manhood

you have gained and think of the glory which you will win for Athens one way or another.'

"That is what my father said. Now this evening my friends will rejoice with me because my son's efforts have made him a young man, when he used to be a child. He need not come with a ribbon on his head to such a feast."

"My father," the boy began, but Conon was afraid he might shed tears.

"It is time to be going," he cried briskly, "or the procession will be starting on its way without us both. Give the oil flask to Sandas to carry for you. Remember, it is only for great occasions. Do not let me find you showing it off in the exercise grounds, or I shall be angry."

Cleitos had pulled himself together, and he smiled at Athenais. "Wish me luck, then; and if the gods will it, I'll bring you the ribbon."

"But his tunic!" said a little voice, protesting. "No one said anything about his tunic!"

"Why, Ala," said Athenais, smiling at her daughter, but shaking her head to reprove her all the same. "Little girls do not speak unasked when men are present."

Aletheia blushed. She was four years younger than her brother and much untidier. Her soft brown hair was plaited in a coronet around her head, but little tendrils were straggling, even this early in the day, across her forehead. Her long, loose robe was awkwardly hitched in her girdle, so that on one side it showed her brown foot and ankle, while on the other it trailed in the dust. But she

had a sweet little face which looked at her father with a shy smile, as though she were not frightened of him.

Conon smiled back. He was proud of his son, but fond of his daughter. Encouraged, the child lifted the doll which she held in the crook of her arm and showed it to him. "I did not say one word. It was Gorgo that spoke."

Conon laughed aloud at that and put out a finger to brush the hair off the child's forehead. Phyllis, whose duty it should have been to help Ala dress, put her own finger into her mouth, looking nervous. But Conon only said lightly, "Then you must teach Gorgo to mind her manners if she wants a husband. But perhaps it was something special that she said."

"Oh yes, it really was. The new tunic that Cleitos has on. I made it all by myself. It took a year."

"Indeed it did," agreed Athenais. "It is Ala's first real piece of cloth; and until we bleached it, there were blood spots on it where the shuttle pricked her finger. And sometimes her arm ached so that she cried, did you not, Ala?"

Conon looked gravely at his daughter. "Then Ala, too, has grown this year. Why, she is almost a maiden already, when I thought she was only a baby. Today is Cleitos's day, and we must hurry-

so that we are not late. But little girls have their day, too, when they are ready for it. I will take Ala to see the bear dance which the priestesses perform for Artemis."

Aletheia gave a little skip of excitement, clutching Gorgo. Except for going with the servants to the well, she had almost never been outside the safe, familiar house; for it was not proper that little girls should be seen by all sorts of strangers. She looked at her mother, wondering what a bear dance was; but Athenais had turned to her husband, saying sadly, "She is so young."

"For Aletheia it is time," said Conon, not unkindly, but in the voice which settled matters in that household.

The
Legend

ALA WOULD HAVE LIKED to ask her mother about the
bear dance; but in the bustle of wishing Cleitos
good luck and fitting on his ivy garland, she knew
better than to raise her voice again. After the men
had gone, there was work to be done before the heat
of the day. Eunice, for instance, had to bake the
dark, sweet honey cakes for which she was famous,
adding nuts and raisins until the mouth watered.
Athenais made a pungent sauce for the fish, which
lay in the storeroom keeping cool in an earthen crock
wetted by the slow drip from a waterskin hung overhead.

Phyllis filled the water jars at the well down-
street, not daring to linger for a gossip today. Dust
and sand were everywhere in the house because the
rooms were open to the courtyards. The women
were sweeping and scrubbing and polishing most
of the morning. The floor of the banquet room,
which was of colored tile with a pattern of leaping

dolphins, was rubbed down with beeswax until it shone. Tables were cleaned, all the best cups put out, and the great bowls for the mixing of wine with water were carefully washed. Phyllis was kept busy bringing water here and there, and she grumbled dreadfully if a jar had to be refilled or a drop was wasted.

Under the colonnade of the men's court lay heaps of myrtle which the menservants had brought in to be made into garlands. There were flowers, too, which must be plunged in water lest they droop in the heat of the day before the party. Athenais broke the seals on a jar of the very best wine and put it ready.

What a feast it was to be! Even in the women's court they were to have their own share of the dates from Asia, of the fine fresh figs, of the olives and plump raisins, of the honey cakes and the goat's milk cheese, and the special pottage delicately flavored with onions and meat broth. They made garlands for themselves; and Athenais brought scented oil from her store so that the servants might have perfume on their hair, for she said, "Eunice is as good as a mother to us all, while Phyllis and Callina work side by side with us and must share in our pleasures."

The sun blazed out of a cloudless sky, so that by ten it was growing warm. At noon they were all glad that the labor was over and they could gather in the shady part of the court to do their spinning. Even Ala had her own distaff with a hank of wool upon it and threw her spindle out and rolled the thread up as neatly as the rest. Only Gorgo, who sat propped against her stool with wooden legs sprawling, stared vacantly with her painted eyes and did nothing.

Often Athenais liked to sing with her girls as they sat at their spinning. She knew an old spinning song comparing the spindle to a dove flying out of a maiden's hand. She taught them ballads, too, and many a love song. Sometimes Callina, who was trained in music, would play for them on the flute. Athenais did not care much for idle gossip, and she only laughed when Eunice said she would rather learn a useful charm to cure warts than all the silly wailings of the poets.

Athenais was not the ordinary housewife with no learning except about charms and magic spells picked up from the chatter of slaves. In the year she had worked on Athene's robe, the maidens of the temple had been in the charge of an old priestess who had served the goddess for endless years

and liked to remind the girls that Athene was goddess of wisdom as well as of weaving. Athene's
daughters, as she used to call them, were made to
learn verses of poets about the old legends and then
to discuss them as men did, picking out the ideas
which lay behind them. They even talked about
what different wise men said about the world, how
it was made of atoms, or fire, or water, or spirit in
various forms. They were set to argue about what
goodness was and how to recognize it.

During the time of this old priestess, the girls of
Athene were known to become wives that a man
could really talk to, not just silly dolls like Gorgo
with nothing in their heads. Conon's father had
thought that he made a great bargain in getting one
for his son. As for Conon, he fell in love with Athenais at their bridal, which was the first time that he
ever saw her. Because of this, he had given her Callina, for whom he had paid a great price. For the
girl was trained in poetry and music and could
even read and write. She came from Ephesus on
the Asia Minor coast, where many women were
taught as carefully as men and showed themselves
openly at banquets as entertainers.

Today as they sat down to spin, Athenais thought
they were all too tired for singing, so she turned

to Callina. "Tell us the story of how Agamemnon, king of many, gathered all the heroes of Greece on the shores of Aulis that they might take ship for Troy to win back Helen, his brother's wife, who had run away with Paris. Tell us, how he slew his own daughter, Iphigenia, as a sacrifice to Artemis to get a fair wind."

Callina had great skill in story telling, and she made them see it all: the black tents huddled along the shore, the green spring grass trampled into mud and cropped by horses, the painted ships side by side on the beach, masts stowed and sails still folded. On the headland the dark king stared at the sea, running high with white spray flying. One day it was gay and blue; the next cold and gray with rain falling in slanting lines from the northeast. But always the same wind blew, straight out of Troy, so that no ship could put to sea until it abated.

Now came the prophet to talk to the king, an old man, tall as Sandas, with a woolen band around his head to mark his office and a long white beard which streamed in the wind. Straight from the sacrifice he came, for sheep and oxen were daily slain, and many prayers were chanted, imploring the high gods to change the wind. In such haste did he

come that his hands were still red from the blood
of the sacrifice, for he had been peering at the en-
trails of the slain beasts, in which messages from
the gods were written for those who could understand them.

The prophet looked the king in the eye and
said, "The gods are angry, and no one but the king
can buy of them a fair wind."

The king laughed aloud. "Then all is well, for there is nothing that I will not give. Rich above all other kings am I, and in my citadel behind the lions which guard my gate lies treasure uncounted. Here our food is half eaten already, and heroes start to grumble that the gods are against us. Presently they will begin to go home and leave me the laughingstock of Greece. I do not care what the gods desire from me. I gladly give it for a fair wind."

The prophet shook his head gloomily. "It is a maiden that calls for a maiden. Moon goddess Artemis is angry, queen of maidens, wild huntress on the hills with the beasts of the nighttime. She will have a girl for her own, your daughter, Iphigenia."

The king spread his hands with a smile. "Why, gladly will I give her, and a dowry with her fit for a princess. I had thought to marry her to Achilles, noblest of heroes; but if she must become a priestess of Artemis, so be it."

The prophet was a bold man, but at this he looked about him as though he wished that some of the heroes were present to save him from the king's anger. But when he saw he stood alone, he gathered his courage and straightened himself to his full height, raising one red hand to heaven.

"It is the huntress who calls. She is goddess of

the panther, and of the bear of the northern hills, and of the wolf pack which howls for blood by night. You shall cut the throat of your daughter, O king, and let her blood run on the altar. Then, only then, will the goddess send a fair wind."

The dark king said nothing for a full minute, but the red of his anger rushed up into his face until it looked swollen and his very eyes were bloodshot. His hand clenched on his sword and drew it half out of its sheath, as though he would have liked to cut down the prophet, even with the bands of his sacred office upon him. It was a plot against him, cried the king, finding voice. Some of the heroes were eager to go home, and they were trying to put the blame upon him. He would have vengeance on such cowards, and on the lying prophet, too, who had surely been promised a great sum of gold to tell this story.

The prophet, glad enough to have done his errand and find himself still alive, went away without another word. The next day and the next the wind still blew, and there was a muttering among the heroes in their tents. The dark king walked alone to the headland and stood gazing out on the pitiless sea. There the heroes came to him, first Odysseus, the clever one with crafty advice, then huge Ajax full of anger because many had come to die for the king, while he in return would give no life from among his own. Next came Achilles, the golden hero, whose goddess mother had whispered that he would not come home from Troy. Menelaos, the king's brother, deserted husband, came in anger, crying that his honor was lost if they did not get back Helen.

Still the wind blew on, and once more Odysseus went up to the headland to pour his advice into the king's ear. Soft and cold were the words of Odysseus, like the snowflakes in winter, smothering hot anger, covering shame, and freezing pity. Presently the dark king nodded, though he groaned as he did it.

A joyful messenger came to the gates of Mycenae, within whose walls the king's proud wife sat on his throne and took counsel with his elders. He bade her dress her daughter for her bridal and send her to the camp straight away for her marriage to Achilles. It was great news for the queen that her daughter should be married to one so glorious and rich, yet she was sad because the kingdom of Achilles lay very far in the north and it was likely that she would not see the girl again. Therefore, though her husband had bidden her stay at home and rule the kingdom, she went to Aulis with the bridal party, glad and sorry as mothers often are on such occasions.

Glorious was the train that carried the king's daughter to her strange bridal. Lovely were her attendants, and vast was her treasure in fine gold work and precious jewels, robes stiff with embroidery, jars of costly perfume, and chests inlaid with ivory. Nothing was lacking which might display the wealth of the king, the pride of the queen, or the greatness of the match.

Gay was their entry into the camp, but grim their reception. The dark king hardly spoke a word, and none of the heroes had the heart to tell the girl what fate awaited. Yet sooner or later it must be done, and done it was.

The poor girl wept, not only for her dreadful fate, but also for the bright hopes of which she had been cruelly cheated. Her mother raged like a lioness whose cubs are taken, vowing that vengeance for the dark deed should overtake her husband. But minds were already made up. The king saw that his honor, perhaps even his kingdom or his life, depended on this wind.

It was not for nothing that Iphigenia had been born the daughter of a great king and kin to the gods. When she had shed tears for her lost youth and the happiness which she would never see, she said she was ready to die for the sake of the host and for the honor of her father. She ordered her attendants to dress her in simple robes that were fitting for a victim; and she walked with steady steps toward the altar where the dark king was waiting with the knife. As she went, she sang a lament. A great poet had written a song she might have used, and Callina sang it, a farewell to her maidenhood forever.

The spindles went on twirling when Callina had finished, but the story was so sad that nobody spoke. After a moment, however, Athenais turned to Eunice, saying, "To my mind King Agamemnon did a terrible wrong. What do you say about it?"

Eunice shook her head hastily. "It is never lucky to talk in that way about the gods and heroes." She made a sign to keep off evil spirits.

"Well, what do you think, Phyllis?"

Phyllis, who never thought at all if she could help it, merely muttered, "Things were different then."

"They were indeed," agreed Athenais kindly, "but good and evil do not change. Remember how vengeance fell on King Agamemnon ten years later when he returned in triumph from Troy. His queen struck him down with an axe as he entered his bath. She in her turn was murdered by her son, on whom the gods sent madness in punishment. Thus one evil deed spread out like an infection through all the family of the dark king."

"It was Artemis who asked for the sacrifice," said Callina scowling. "Why should we blame the king?"

"But did she really call for it?" demanded Athenais. "Who knows why wind changes or what the gods may mean? Maybe the prophet was mistaken, or maybe Artemis was only trying the temper of the king. At all events, we know that when the heroes looked at the body on the altar, thinking they saw the maiden, they really saw a fawn. For Artemis had lifted the girl away in a cloud and left an animal to be killed in her place." She looked at Ala, who was listening eagerly and frowning as she tried to puzzle out the meaning of the story. "Shall I tell you the rest of it?"

"Oh yes."

"Well, far to the north of us lies the land of the Taurians, a savage country full of dark woods, and bears, and beasts of prey, and fierce eagles. The barbarians who live there worship Artemis, because the huntress is powerful in wild places. There

they had built a great and gloomy temple as a home for an image which had fallen from heaven in distant times. Here the goddess sent Iphigenia to be her own priestess."

"From princess to a slave of the goddess," cried Callina angrily. "For my part, I would sooner have poured my blood across the altar. But the kindnesses of the gods are selfish ones. They care nothing for us."

"Poor Callina," said Athenais softly. Her slavery was hateful to Callina, and this was strange because she was born to it. But then she had been trained as an entertainer, so that the dullness of the women's court and the silly chatter of the female slaves got on her nerves.

Callina hunched her shoulders and looked sulky. She did not like being pitied.

"It is true that Iphigenia was not happy," Athenais said. "How should she be so, far from her own land and amid savage people? But Callina thinks too much about happiness and too little about the wise purposes of the gods. It was the custom among the Taurians that any stranger who came into their land through shipwreck, or by travel, or indeed in any way was sacrificed to the image of Artemis which had fallen from heaven.

"Be sure that Iphigenia hated this custom. How could she do anything else, being what she was? But nothing she could say would alter the old ways, though to my thinking the goddess may have carried her there for that purpose. Every so often the priestess was called to purify a new victim whose blood was to flow before the image.

"Time went by in the land of the Taurians, and nothing was changed. But out in the rest of the world, Troy was taken, and King Agamemnon came home in triumph — to his death. Years passed again, and the queen's son, Orestes, came home from a far country whither he had been secretly sent by his father's friends, and slew his mother in vengeance for the murder of his father."

"And serve her right," Eunice lifted hands of horror. "A woman kill her husband! What should we come to next?"

"So the gods thought, I daresay," Athenais agreed. "Yet it is an evil thing for a child to kill his mother. Thus the gods punished Orestes with terrible visions and drove him almost to madness. Yet at the same time they told him that if he would do a great deed for them, they would grant him forgiveness. The task they laid on him was that he should rescue the image of Artemis from the Taurian land, so that her altar need no longer be stained with the blood of men.

"Orestes took ship for Tauris, but he dared not land openly there, lest he too be slain for the goddess. He hid his ship in a cove and went ashore with one comrade to see where the image was and how he might steal it. But while they were prowling around, they were discovered, bound with ropes, and dragged into the temple so that the priestess might purify them before the killing.

"Orestes did not recognize his sister, nor yet she him, because the maiden had been fully fourteen years old when she went to Aulis, while he had been an infant in his cradle. It was many years, however, since a Greek had come to Tauris; and she was hungry for news. She did not even know that Troy was taken, much less that her father was dead; that noble Achilles, who was to have married her, had perished also; or that Odysseus, who had counseled her death, was wandering across the sea, no man knew where or whither. Thus through question and answer she learned the truth, that her brother Orestes, who had taken this guilt on himself, now stood before her, the heir of their noble line, but the goddess's victim.

"Many tears were shed and kisses were given

before they made a plot to escape and take the image with them. First the priestess called the king of Tauris and told him that one of the strangers was a man guilty of murder and must be washed clean in seawater with very secret rites. What made the whole thing worse, she said, was that the image had been touched by his hand and must be washed as well. She wanted to take the prisoners, bound, hobbled, yet able to walk, down onto the seashore, together with the image. But nobody must watch what she did.

"The king agreed, for he was afraid of the goddess and saw no reason not to trust the priestess. But he did not like to leave her alone with two male prisoners, even if they were bound with ropes. He was afraid of the secret rites, but he was even more frightened lest harm be done to the holy image. Pretending to go away, he hid behind a big rock in case he was needed.

"When he saw that the priestess had cut the men loose and that a warship with fifty rowers aboard had come around the headland and was racing for the shore, he knew he had been cheated. He gave a great shout and rushed after the fugitives, who were wading into the surf toward the ship. Hearing his cry, a mob of Taurians with drawn swords in their hands came rushing after.

"Then the three would have been killed, but Pallas Athene, who was watching over them, sped on the rowers. Men leaped into the sea to seize the princess and hoist the image aboard. Others threw out ropes to drag in Orestes and his faithful comrade. Archers sent arrows whizzing about the Taurians' ears."

"They were safe," cried Ala, dropping her spindle to the ground in her excitement. "They were safe and the poor princess could go home."

Athenais looked at her with a little smile. "Not home, dear Ala. She had been so long away and, you see, her parents were dead. She came to Athens, where she made a temple for the image which you will visit someday. Athens was always a kindly place. King Theseus, whose feast it is today, had made it a refuge for unhappy folk and a pleasant place to live in. Even the image was glad to make a home in Athens, instead of in Tauris."

Ala shook her head distressed. She did not much like this end to the story. It was not pleasant to think of that bloodstained image in Athens.

"You must not be frightened of the image," Athenais said. "Today people offer cakes and wine and little things before her altar. Artemis never needed the blood of men to make her happy. Here she is the protector of little girls like you, too young to marry. Indeed, there is only one thing about the image which reminds us that she is strange and has a history. She likes to think just now and then of the woods and hills of Tauris, and perhaps of the king's brave daughter who was her priestess. For this reason, we dance a bear dance for her yearly to remind her how the bears prowl on the moonlit hills of distant Tauris."

Ala looked at her mother with a wide smile of purest pleasure. "Why, Artemis is my goddess, and this was my story, to tell me of the bear dance!"

Athenais nodded. "And to pass the time on this long day. Cleitos will have run his race by now, and presently Sandas will slip away home to tell us what happened. We had better put away our spinning and make ourselves fine. It is a day of rejoicing for the whole house, not just for the men's quarters."

There was a shouting in the men's court, and old Sandas came hurrying in. "Victory, Mistress! He won! The gods were on our side because young Phormio slipped in the sand at the start. Our dear master ran like the son of a champion that he is."

Everybody clapped and cried out. Ala jumped off her stool to prance through the court, forgetting Gorgo. Even Callina really smiled for once and ordered Sandas to tell them all about it from the beginning. Only Athenais, who had a good word for everyone, exclaimed, "Oh poor Phormio! How he must be feeling!"

"Bother Phormio!" snapped Eunice, forgetting her manners. "A boy you never saw! Who cares for him when our own darling's crowned with ribbon!"

Athenais let them all chatter as they pleased, but she kissed Eunice.

The
Bear
Dance

———

"What's a bear?" demanded Ala shrilly. "Cleitos, Cleitos, what's a bear?" She tugged at his tunic.

"Let go," said Cleitos crossly, pulling away. "A bear's an animal, you silly girl."

"Silly yourself!" retorted Ala. "You think girls don't know *anything!* I mean, what's a bear like? Eunice said you saw one."

"Well, I did," Cleitos agreed. "There was a traveling man who brought one to Athens. He had it on a rope, and when his boy played on a flute, it stood up on its hind legs and danced."

"It did? You saw it dance? Really dance like this?" Ala made a few leaps around the courtyard, trying to think how a bear would dance.

"Of course not." Cleitos was still cross. "He was as tall as our father when he stood up, and ever so heavy, a great clumsy brute. Do leave me alone!"

"Well, then, like this?" Ala persisted. "Cleitos, Cleitos! Was it like this?"

"No, it wasn't," snapped Cleitos, losing his temper. "He had great paws with long, sharp claws, and he waved them in the air like this. And he had a great mouth hanging open with a great red tongue and enormous teeth to bite with. Grrr!"

"Stop it!" cried Ala, pushing him off. "Stop it, Cleitos!"

"Grrr!"

"Leave the child alone!" Eunice came bustling forward. "Shame on you for teasing her, and you think yourself a young man!"

"Don't speak to me like that, you . . . you slave!" Cleitos swung his hand and slapped Eunice on the cheek.

Eunice put her hand up to her face and said nothing. Phyllis, who was dipping some water out of a jar, dribbled some of the precious stuff onto the ground as she stared at Cleitos. Athenais, who was sitting nearby with her sewing, said sadly, "Yes, Cleitos, Eunice is our servant; and you are the only person in the house who ever hit her."

Cleitos looked as though he was not certain whether to fly into a rage or burst into tears. "She ought to mind her manners," he shouted, "and not treat me as if . . . as if I were a baby!" He caught sight of Phyllis with the cup in her hand, still spilling water. "Don't stare at me like that, you . . . you," he choked on the word, "you *women!*" With a sudden movement, he rushed out of the court.

"You must not mind him," Athenais said to Eunice, who still stood with her hand pressed to her

cheek. "He is too old for school and not quite ready to do his military service, so that he is neither a boy nor a young man. He does not know where he belongs and feels left out of things. Growing is always pain as well as pleasure."

"I nursed him in my arms," Eunice said. "I sat up nights with him when he had the fever."

"Oh, Eunice," Athenais said, "you know he did not mean it."

"She forgot she was a slave," said Callina bitterly, "and she had to be reminded."

Athenais made no answer. There were moments when it was wiser to say nothing to Callina. Instead, she turned to Ala. "It is time for you to sit down to your weaving. And, Ala, do not tease your brother just now. He cannot bear it."

Ala wiped her eyes on a fold of her dress and sniffed. "I was only asking about the bear."

"Callina shall draw you a picture of one," promised Athenais.

Callina did draw a picture, but it was disappointing. As she confessed, she had never seen a bear herself and could only remember a painting which she had once seen of a bear and a lion. She drew them both, but they did not look very different to Ala, except that the lion had a tail, while the bear had none. Athenais said it did not really matter because the priestesses were not dressed up in bearskins, which would have been too hot and might perhaps have frightened children. It would be better for Ala to wait and see the bear dance for herself.

"But what is it *like?*" persisted Ala.

Athenais smiled. "It is a mystery for little girls. Men never go until they take their daughters. Women who have seen it do not talk about it to those who have not. It is for a time when you are old enough to bring your own gift to the goddess. I will teach you a hymn that we sing then, but the rest you must see for yourself."

Conon had said no more about his promise, but nobody thought he had forgotten it. Half a dozen times a day Eunice said, "You must braid your hair better, or your father will be ashamed to take you out. What will your father think if you go out on the street with your girdle badly knotted? How can you be fit to be seen if you get your gown so dirty?" There were times when Ala felt nearly as cross with Eunice as Cleitos had been.

What made the fuss more tiresome was that in the end the women had no idea of letting their darling go out looking untidy. Ala's soft brown hair was washed and braided for her, and even treated with egg white, which made it too stiff to straggle. She was given a new robe, plain white just like the old one, but clean and without creases so that Phyllis, who had neat fingers, could arrange it in folds which Ala was sternly forbidden to crumple.

She felt excited, but solemn. There had been such a scrubbing of nails, such a washing and inspecting. Ten days earlier, Eunice had taken a pattern of her foot and actually gone down to the shoemaker for sandals. They felt strange and heavy, while the stiff straps raised blisters on her feet. Eunice made her wear them a little every day, but they never grew quite comfortable. Eunice said that was just as well. They would remind her not to skip or jump as she walked beside her father.

There is a queer thing about going anywhere, which Ala discovered on this day. You start it just where you always live. You walk across the men's courtyard, and the porter opens the door, and you go down the street toward the well, just the same way that you have gone a thousand times with Phyllis or Eunice. Only this time you have your sandals on, which are creaking. You are holding on to your father's cloak and feeling strange because you are not stopping at the well, and because you know one of the neighbor's women who is coming up with her jar, but you are not certain if you ought to smile at her today or not. She is only a slave.

Ala started to smile and then saw that she had done the wrong thing because the woman stood aside for her father, looking as though she did not know there was anybody with him. Ala blushed and turned away her face. Luckily she did not have much time to feel awkward. They went past the well and plunged into a new world.

It might not have been very different if Eunice had not given so many warnings. Ala hid her face in her father's cloak, quite certain everybody was staring at her, saying, "There's a little girl on the street. Look at her! I wonder how well she has been brought up by her father and mother."

It was late in the day, but the narrow streets were crowded with men coming back from exercise or slaves on errands, with peasants who, though market was long over, had lingered on to gossip and were now starting home with empty baskets or unladen donkeys. When a flock of goats came down the street, Ala and her father had to step aside into the doorway of a shop, whose owner darted out to catch Conon by the arm, shrieking loudly, "Buy a lucky charm for the maid of Artemis! Buy a bracelet for her dower chest! Tell your fortune, pretty maiden, noble lord! Just one obol! Only one copper coin for all the widom of the East!"

Conon pushed him off and left him screaming curses which made Ala shrink back against her fa-

ther. Conon paid no attention, and presently the shrill cries were drowned by other vendors and by the growing din of hammers on metal from the quarter of the armorers, still busy at the end of the long day. Ala gained courage to look around and began to see that nobody was watching. Indeed, whenever a friend stopped to greet Conon, he did not notice Ala by the slightest flicker of an eye. The most he ever said was "Going to the dancing?" which he might easily have guessed because behind Conon came one of the outdoor slaves to light them homeward.

The dancing was held on the Acropolis rock in the center of the city, on the top of which gleamed the marble temple of Athene. As they came to the foot of the path which led up to this, Conon was stopped by another friend. The two men stood chatting for a moment while two little girls, each clutching a fold of her father's mantle, peeped at one another.

Ala gave the ghost of a timid smile. The other deliberately closed and opened one of her blue eyes in a big wink.

Ala looked hastily away. She was not quite certain whether the poor thing did not have a twitch in her eye; but when she looked back to make sure, she distinctly saw the other giggle.

Nothing Eunice had said, and she had said plenty, covered this situation. Ala clapped her hand over her mouth in case she might be tempted to giggle back. Luckily before worse happened, the men strolled uphill together, dividing their daughters by their two large persons.

There were plenty of other girls going up to the dancing, tall and short, plain and pretty, well cared for and ragged. Some glanced about them boldly, especially the country lasses burned brown by helping in the fields; but all of them looked solemn, as if they knew what fitted the occasion.

At the top of the hill, on the great staircase which led up to the sacred places stood men selling flat cakes colored yellow with saffron and shaped like birds or little animals. While Conon was buying a fawn for Ala to offer the goddess, she caught sight of the other little girl around her father. Immediately the child put fingers at the corners of her mouth, nose, and eyes, stretching them hideously. She put her tongue out.

Before Ala could decide what to do in return, Conon bent to give her the cake, saying, "Ala, remember this gift to the goddess is a token that you are her maiden and that one day you must offer a greater gift of your own."

Ala felt solemn again as she carefully nodded.

The dancing place lay before the sanctuary of Artemis, but though the goddess had her holy spot on the Acropolis and her stone image in the stiff style of earlier days, the wooden image which had once fallen from heaven did not dwell there. She lived at Brauron on the coast and sent out her high priestess, in whom the spirit of Iphigenia still dwelt, to bless the dancing. This year it was the great feast, the four-year one. Iphigenia would lead a vast procession back to Brauron for a secret ritual, a Mystery, which would be celebrated by games and recitations.

Ala looked around her curiously. Behind the dancing place and a little to one side stood a booth thickly covered with green laurel and hung with garlands. Before it smoked an altar burning pine logs, whose scent was especially pleasing to the goddess. The sun was going down, and although torches had been kindled all around the dancing place, Ala could only see the high priestess dimly, sitting enthroned inside the booth and still as a statue.

There was no sign of any bears. Before the altar stood a tall, straight priestess with the woolen bands of her office around her head. Other priestesses were moving through the crowd collecting the yellow cakes in wide rush baskets. Ala laid hers on the top and saw it taken straight up to the altar. Here the priestess took one and crumbled it over the flame, praying that Artemis would look with favor on her worshipers. Then the basket was set aside with others in front of the booth.

The sun lay low on the horizon, glowing like a fiery ball as it slid its rim beneath the circle of hills that fringed the western plain. The crowd was massing around the dancing place, so that Conon lifted Ala onto his shoulders for a better view.

Slowly the high priestess arose, hands out before her with palms up. Stiff and straight, she began to move forward until she stood outside the booth. She wore a great crown on her head almost a foot tall, while her garment had the pinched waist and wide, flounced skirt of ancient days. It was of white and silver, and the priestess's skin had been whitened until she appeared more like an image than a woman.

Thus she stood facing the crowd for a long moment in which all sound was hushed except the twittering of the sparrows that nested on Athene's temple. As the sun dipped out of sight, she turned to the east where the rugged bulk of Mount Hymettos rose against the sky. She lifted her hands and began to chant a prayer.

There were many things to say to Artemis, for she had many names and shapes and functions. She was bright Phoebe, sister of Apollo, swinging in her moon chariot over the earth. She was the huntress of the dark hills and the leader of dancing nymphs in moonlit glades. When Artemis was angry, arrows of disease sped from her silver bow; or at her summons, wolves slipped down from the north to prowl the sheepfolds. Yet she who harmed could also heal. She was goddess of childbirth, easing the pains of labor for woman or beast. Shepherds and goatherds prayed to her for the welfare of their flocks. Under her protection were the young of men and animals, but most especially unmarried girls. Some legends whispered that she had to do with the birth of spring and the death of old winter. Storms were hers to some extent, for the moon seasons have much to do with weather; and it was no accident that King Agamemnon must buy from her a change of wind.

All these things Artemis was, so that without her

favor neither men, nor flocks, nor even the fruitful
earth could be blessed. But she was also the dread
goddess who had seen much blood, and in whose
honor women used to dance, so the old tales said, in
foaming frenzy. Even now she drank the blood of
goats, so that many a herdsman who hardly tasted
meat all year was feasting this evening on a young
kid from his flock slain in honor of the goddess.

The glow of the sunset faded from the sky, and
presently the evening star shone out. In the silence
which followed the end of the long prayer, a little
flute began to play in the shadows and was
answered by another and another. On either side
of the booth there were shepherds sitting on rocks
which lay tumbled about. Each of them had his
staff at his feet and his faithful dog beside him.

"They are playing up the moon," whispered
Conon to Ala.

There was indeed a glow behind Hymettos as the
stars came out one by one and the sky darkened.
Shrilly the pipes called to one another, appealing,
crying, joining in harmony as the bright disk of the
moon rose into sight.

Not until it was fully up, shedding its pale light
over the marble of Athene's gleaming temple and
making the circle beside the torches seem almost

bright as day, did anything happen. Shadows began to stir behind the booth which housed the image. One by one, lurching as they walked and pawing at the air, the bears came in.

Ala felt a pang of disappointment. The priestesses were only little girls, who looked quite comic as they tried to walk like something big and clumsy. Each came forward into the light and turned in a little circle, displaying her costume, while the audience hummed in applause.

They were all dressed in robes of a bright yellow with long sleeves covering their arms and furry mittens ending in black claws. Each wore a bear mask, covering her head completely. The first head was large and black, the second rounder and yellowish-brown. One mouth lolled open in a grin with pink tongue drooping; another snarled, revealing cruel teeth. The next had a bent ear, jagged from some old wound. There was gray on her muzzle. Behind her came the smallest one of all, a furry cub. Each bear in fact was different from the others.

They did not dance at first, but simply plodded with their swaying gait around in a full circle. Then one began to pat at another, pushing clumsily till she fell against a third, who thrust her back. The

circle broke up into groups which wrestled together, still in slow motion. Now and then one
would sit down with a thump; getting up again, she
would throw her arms about another's shoulders.

A tall black bear with a great red tongue in front
of Ala was climbing onto the shoulders of three
others, who made a circle for her with their arms.
She stood upright, swaying to the music and beating the air with her hands while they carried her
around the dancing place with the other bears lum-
bering after.

The pipes began to play faster; the pyramid of
bears moved into the middle and began to turn
there in a tight circle with the other bears dancing
around it. As their speed increased, the black bear
leaped from their shoulders with a wild cry and fell
lightly, feet already moving in the complicated patterns of a dance.

Now they were no longer tame bears shuffling
awkwardly through drilled paces, but wild bears,
leaping, hurling themselves through undergrowth,
just as a great stone, forerunner of an avalanche,
goes bounding straight down the side of a rocky
mountain. Faster than the horse is the wild bear,
faster even than a stag pursued by hounds. When he
dances for the goddess, great muscles ripple be-

neath his glossy hide. Leaping, twisting, circling madly, now twirling in twos and threes, now rushing together, now scattering to the edges of the circle, the little bear priestesses danced to the moon.

Now and again they would halt for a few minutes, chests heaving, while one of their number danced in the center of the circle with nimble feet on the white sand. Presently the music called, and at first slowly, then ever faster and faster they joined in the dance.

People were throwing them bunches of flowers. The bears tossed them about or tore them asunder and scattered them on the sand. The torches were

dying, and the flower heads looked black in the moonlight. At the edge of the dancing place, spectators were swaying in time to the music. Now and then a voice raised the wild wolf call which signals that the huntress with her dogs is abroad in the hills.

Men began to sing, "O Artemis, goddess of mothers, daughter of Leto, dance on the mountains, as your delicate locks fly streaming in the wind."

Many voices joined in, the deep bass of men mingled with childish trebles.

"Moon goddess, queen of the silver bow, brought hither by a daughter of kings to dwell in kindly Athens,

"Protectress of maidens, long may you live in your white temple near the sea and watch over our land."

The music died away, and it was over. Conon lifted Ala from his shoulder and set her on the ground. She clung to him, shivering a little with excitement and perhaps with cold. Conon stroked her hair. "Did you like the dancing, Ala?"

She took a long breath. It had been so beautiful that she did not know what to say. Her eyes were still full of pictures of yellow robes flying, white sand, black masks, and silver moonlight. She was thinking that it was no wonder that the protectress of maidens in her white temple loved the bears to dance.

Conon was saying something else, but her head was so full of these thoughts that she did not understand it until he looked at her in surprise and suddenly his words flashed into her mind.

"Next year," Conon had said, "it will be time for

you to dance the bear dance yourself. Will you like it?"

"Oh," gasped Ala, quite overwhelmed, "can I do *that?*"

The
Journey

About ten days after the bear dance, Conon came home from market with a wicker cage in which, looking cautiously at Ala out of a bright pink eye, sat a bird.

"Mine? Really mine?" Ala could hardly believe it. He was so pretty with the shiny pinks and purples of his neck, his blue-gray wings, the black band of his tail, his neat pink legs. She put a finger into the cage, just a little way, but he took no notice.

"You must offer him a seed," said Athenais.

"Take care of him, Ala. He is your special gift to Artemis," warned Conon.

Ala drew back her finger quickly, and her face fell. To sacrifice animals to the gods was as natural as breathing. When the farmer came to kill his beast in the fall, he always made a feast of the occasion, offering the creature to his god. Thriftily he burned on the altar the inner parts which he did not eat himself, pleasing the god with the smell and depriving nobody except the hungry vultures who feed on refuse. But the farmer's daughter who had made a pet of a special lamb wept when the time for slaughter came, as farmers' daughters always have and will. Far wiser, she thought, would she have been not to love the creature.

Ala felt this, too; and yet she was tempted. Surely she might offer the bird one seed! He was so pretty; and then he was her own, at least for the moment.

"How soon must I give him to Artemis?" she asked cautiously.

"Not until you wish," Conon promised. "He is yours for as long as you choose."

Athenais sighed and said softly, "Remember growing is pain as well as pleasure." But Ala, who had heard this piece of wisdom before, took no notice of it.

"He took it!" she shrieked, excited. "Did you see him? He took the seed right out of my fingers!"

"He is hungry, I daresay," suggested Conon. "You must give him food and water. When he knows you, we will clip his wings so that he cannot fly away. Then you may have him out of his cage when you please."

Ala gave a long sigh of pleasure. "What shall I call him?"

Conon thought a moment. "Solon, I think," he said, "because Solon was a wise man. Aletheia means truth, and truth must go with wisdom."

"Solon, Solon!" called Aletheia. She whistled gently; and Solon nodded his head as pigeons do, and he cooed.

From this time Gorgo was left in a dark corner, while Solon rode everywhere on Ala's shoulder. Phyllis grumbled because he messed upon it sometimes, but Athenais only smiled. Never was a bird so stroked and petted, so spoiled with fresh water for his birdbath, so whistled for, so coaxed with seeds, which Ala taught him to take from between her lips. In the night, his cage sat beside her bed. If she dreamed sometimes that he belonged to Artemis, at least on waking she could say to herself, "Not till I want to give him. Not till I choose!" Deep down in her heart, where even goddesses do not listen, she whispered, "I will never choose."

It was all very well to say this, but inside herself Ala had a feeling that someday she would have to fight for Solon.

"Are you growing deaf or sulky?" grumbled Eunice. "Why won't you ever answer nowadays?"

Ala opened her eyes in surprise. "I didn't hear you. I was thinking."

She had plenty to think about because ever since the bear dance and the coming of Solon, life had been changing. To dance the bear dance, Athenais said, one must be a priestess. In the valley of Brauron down by the coast where the image dwelt in its white temple, it was served yearlong by little girls. Here they learned the ancient prayers, wove garlands for the goddess, washed her sacred vessels, practiced her dances, and obeyed the old priestesses. So gently did Athenais explain the matter that Ala only gradually understood that she was going away. She would live in the temple of Artemis for a whole year without Eunice or Phyllis or Callina, or her mother and father, or even Cleitos, who so seldom came into the women's court anymore. She was going alone.

Ala looked around the little court with tears in her eyes. She had always known that when she was fourteen or fifteen, a really grown-up girl, Conon would arrange a marriage. She did not dread this because she expected to feel quite different at fourteen, which was in any case far in the future. But by now she was already twelve and was going to spend a year in the temple of Artemis. Why, even when she came home, she would soon have to leave forever. Ala felt cheated. She longed to cuddle down into the old familiar ways, but nobody would let her.

"I don't think I want to dance the bear dance after all." She sniffed.

Athenais put an arm around her. "You may wait till next year if you wish. Would you rather do so?"

But Ala, who had been crying because she did not want to leave home, now sobbed harder because life at the temple would be an adventure she did not like to miss.

"If you were going to live here all your life like poor Phyllis," explained Athenais, "it might be better for you never to go out. One day you will live in another house with different people and will have slaves of your own. It will be easier to fall in with new ways if you have seen something of strangers."

Ala nodded. She did not want to talk, only to let Athenais hold her. Presently she lifted her head. "May I take Solon?"

"Why, Solon goes wherever you go," Athenais told her.

After this it was settled that Ala should go to the

temple; but even when Conon had arranged the matter, it did not prove easy to make a journey of more than twenty miles. Conon could have taken Ala in front of him on his horse and, with a servant behind him on a donkey with her gear, would have carried her to Brauron without trouble. It happened, however, that the Athenians had cause of complaint against their Theban neighbors about some goats which had been raided across the border. Envoys were to be sent about this and other questions. For such business, no one could be better than an Olympic victor whose name was known to every Greek and whose reputation for wisdom was steadily growing.

For this reason Conon was absent, but he was anxious that Ala's visit to the temple be not delayed. This meant that she must go in the cart which the women used on their rare visits to the country.

"I shall have to send for one of the farm servants," said Athenais unhappily. "Sandas is too old to help on a rough road; and all the others except for Lydios are with the master. You'll go, Eunice."

Eunice nodded grimly. She did not fancy jolting forty miles in a springless cart, but the mistress must not travel without her husband, while the daughter of the house must be escorted by a

respectable woman. Phyllis was too young for such work, and Callina not to be relied on.

Eunice was to go, but her presence merely added to the difficulties of the trip. Conon on horseback could have gone and returned in a day. The men-servants would have thought nothing of sleeping one night on the ground, but Eunice was getting stiff in the joints. Athenais had made up her mind that a night out would not do for Eunice. The difficulty was that friends of the family who would have been glad to do a favor for Conon were not known to Athenais. Besides, they would think it odd to trouble themselves about the sleeping quarters of a slave in summer. Cleitos, whom Athenais consulted in the matter, was sure he would be laughed at.

"Then you will have to go yourself," said Athenais. "There is no reason why you should not visit your father's friends and bring the servants."

Cleitos considered this idea with favor. His father had left him in charge of the household, so that he was delighted to have a chance of showing how well he could manage. Besides, he had been attending lectures in mathematics from a famous wise man who was visiting Athens. They had not proved as easy as he hoped, and he was happy to take a holiday for a couple of days in the country.

The matter being thus arranged, they set out early one morning before the heat of the day. Cleitos went ahead, riding bareback, as the custom was, on a horse which his father had given him against the day when he was ready to join the cavalry. At the tail of the procession trudged a strong young man from the farm, whose job was to help the cart over rough places. In the middle came Lydios driving the mule cart, whose canopy and curtains made it clear to lookers-on that the ladies of the house were taking a journey.

Inside the cart, it was crowded. Eunice, perched stiffly on the board which was used for a seat, was trying to wedge herself with the cushions which Athenais had pressed upon her. Aletheia, whose eyes were red, was still crying as she tried to get Solon's cage between her own legs and the chest she was taking with her, containing her other robe and warm cloak, a rough wool blanket, her comb and hairpins, a mirror of polished bronze given her by Athenais, a set of ribbons woven by Phyllis, a pretty necklace of earthenware beads painted in bright colors by Callina, and a vial full of a bitter medicine which Eunice had brewed for fevers and troublesome coughs and stomachache and other ailments.

The curtains of the cart were not tight, so that it was possible to get a glimpse of the streets; and Eunice promised that out in the country, they might be drawn back. Ala began to cheer up. Sad though she felt to think of Athenais sitting in the dear, dusty court, it was impossible to waste her first journey in crying. Presently their progress down the narrow street was halted by a donkey coming the other way, so laden with brush to be sold for fuel that he appeared to be nothing but the bottoms of four legs trotting under his burden. There was no question of either passing the other, and a dispute arose between Cleitos and the man in charge of the donkey, an elderly peasant who did not see any reason why he should give way to a rich boy on a horse. Excitement mounted as people hurried up to join in the quarrel. Ala watched with an eye glued to the gap in the curtain until Cleitos, unwilling to involve his womenfolk in a battle, gave the sign to back the cart amid cries of triumph from the peasant and his supporters.

In the country with the curtains open, it was exciting to see the gray-green olives and the vineyards loaded with ripening grapes. It was not a season in which there was much field work, but here and there a peasant had ridden out from his village on a donkey who was getting a free meal from the grass by the highway. At the end of the day, the peasant's prunings and gleanings would be loaded on his beast and brought home for fuel. Ahead rose Mount Hymettos, purple with heather and dotted with the hives of the beekeepers which made it famous. Gulls squawked overhead while, so high up that he seemed smaller than they, an eagle lazily circled. Ala was busy asking questions of Lydios, while Eunice clung to the sides of the cart, wincing as it jolted through the ruts.

Eunice was not enjoying the trip; and her dislike of it was shared by Cleitos, though for different reasons. It had taken him longer than he had expected to escort the clumsy cart through the streets of Athens. Outside, he had heaved a sigh of relief, only to find that they must go at a slow footpace to spare Eunice. If this was to be true where the road was in constant use, how was he ever to get around the foothills of Hymettos, where the ground was steep and tracks much rougher? Rather sharply he told Lydios not to dawdle, but Lydios grumbled that it would waste more time to break a wheel.

They straggled across the plain, winding in and out between farms, around sacred olives, over barren bits of heath whose thorny clumps of gorse defied even goats. Presently the ground grew hilly. Up and down bumped the cart so that often the farmhand was called to put a shoulder to a wheel, or even to clear loose stones from the path while the others waited.

They rested in the heat of the day in a valley between Hymettos and the sea, looking out over blue water to the wooded peak of Aegina. Eunice had brought barley water for the journey, which she thought more refreshing than wine in this heat. Presently it was time to turn inland to cross to Brauron on the opposite coast.

Things went better after this. They were behind Hymettos, and for a while at least the ground was less rugged. It was afternoon, and they still had a few miles to go; but Lydios said that when they came to the river, the road would be easy.

Eunice tried to look cheerful. Ala was watching some men who were hunting on the side of a rough hill. They had three or four dogs with them in full cry after a hare, which ran dodging from side to side, while the huntsmen, armed with clubs, were trying to drive it into a net which they had stretched across a thicket. So thrilled was she by the chase that she paid no attention when Lydios reined up the mule with a hearty curse.

The path had wound for some time beside a dry stream bed which separated straggling patches of fenced land. One of the owners, more grasping than the rest, had decided to push the road right into the stream, which probably only ran for a few days every time it rained on Hymettos. He had piled up his wall of stones right to the bank and had then planted what once had been the road with cabbages.

Lydios got out and went down into the stream bed. It had been used as a path for some time by men and donkeys, who had cleared loose stones from a track in the middle by edging them away to the sides. This made it worse for the cart, whose arrival on this stretch of road seemed unexpected.

"Best do some work on this," grunted Lydios, summoning the farmhand and starting to move the stones which floods had piled on one another. Cleitos, as interested as Ala in the hunt, which had after furious shouting lost its quarry, climbed up to stand on the cart for a better view.

"They are going to try over there." He pointed. "If we are lucky, we shall pass quite close to them. I'd like to see them kill."

"Oh no!" cried Ala anxiously; but Cleitos merely grinned.

"Look!" he exclaimed. "I told you so. They've found him again."

Lydios came back up the bank. "It's not far, Master, and we will take the cart slowly; but Eunice and the little mistress had best walk."

Ala sprang joyfully down, lifting out Solon, who did not seem to like the shaking either. Eunice, pleading her bad leg, refused to move. She thought it her duty to look after Ala's chest, which ought not to arrive at the temple banged to pieces.

"Look, see!" cried Cleitos. "There! He's slipped them again!" Dogs and huntsmen were streaming down the slope in full cry toward a thicket which seemed to stretch along the stream opposite the cabbages.

"Better lead your horse, Master," said Lydios; and Cleitos, restored to a sense of his duty, got down from the cart.

Lydios started the cart down the bank. It tilted first one way, then the other, while Eunice struggled with the chest. The farmhand panted and heaved, and was abused.

Progress upstream was noisy and uncomfortable, but at least the cart was strongly built. Lydios, shouting at his mule, was telling it between whacks that they would soon be on better ground. Cleitos, coming down the bank with his horse, was yelling instructions, while Eunice, whenever she got her breath, was doing the same. The farmhand, trying in vain to satisfy three people, only grunted. Now and then as he straightened up, he seemed to catch the eye of the mule; and when he did so, he shook his head at it, as though in warning.

They stuck on the lip of a rock which was too deeply embedded to be rolled aside. Lydios thwacked stoutly and cursed. What with the barking of the dogs, who were by now in the thicket, and the shouts of the huntsmen crashing after, the valley was as noisy as an Athenian street.

"Look!" screamed Ala.

Out of the thicket burst the hare with the dogs in full cry after him. He leaped down the low bank into the stream bed, paused for a minute at the sight of the wall on the opposite side, and turned to double upstream. But already one of the huntsmen stood in his path, while the dogs, encouraged by his second of delay, were right on his heels. Swiftly he reversed to dart downstream past the very legs of the mule and under the cart. The dogs followed.

The mule had put up with a good deal. He was used to being yelled at and urged along with a stick, but Lydios had been beating him beyond reason. He disliked a furry animal under his feet, and the dogs were just too much. He tucked down his head, and he kicked.

Crash!

"Jump!" yelled Lydios to Eunice. He suited the action to the word and jumped himself.

Crash! Eunice screamed.

This time the mule got the traces tangled in his legs and fell over sideways, breaking a shaft and jerking Eunice and the chest out of the cart. The farmhand came leaping around the other side and sat on the mule's head. This seemed for some reason to quiet him, and presently Lydios was able to cut him loose.

The hare and the dogs were already in the distance with most of the hunters panting after, but the young man in the stream bed came down to look at the wreckage. He whistled slightly, taking in Ala, who was bending over Eunice; Cleitos, too busy with his horse to be of any help; and the men with the mule.

"You were going to the temple, as I suppose," said he.

Cleitos scowled, unsure of himself. The accident had not been his fault, but it had put him in an awkward position. He felt it his duty to protect his sister from the notice of young strangers.

"My horse will make the journey in an hour I daresay," he answered stiffly, refusing to mention Ala. "The servants can get the cart repaired while I do my errand."

"Cleitos," called Ala from the cart. "Eunice's hurt."

"Be quiet!" snapped Cleitos, angry at having to

draw her into the conversation. "Lydios, you'll
have to look after Eunice."

Lydios shook his head doubtfully. "It's her knee,
Master. We might carry her somewhere between us,
but there's the mule."

Cleitos looked at the mule, who was now on his
feet staring around him with a red and evil eye. No
use supposing that Eunice would consent to sit on

his back. "Well, you'll have to manage, Lydios," he said weakly. "Get up, Ala. We're going on."

He tried to speak as his father would have done, but Aletheia was not afraid of her brother. "It's *Eunice!*" she said boldly. "Cleitos, I'll not go away and leave Eunice hurt."

The young man smiled. He was a few years older than Cleitos, thickset and not handsome, but he had a pleasant smile. "I have an old nurse myself," he remarked. "So, as it's *Eunice,* I think we had better put her on your horse and take her to our farm. My mother lives in Athens, but the tenant who manages for us has a wife and maids. Very likely they will know how to make *Eunice* comfortable."

This was all politely said, but there was a twinkle in the young man's eye. Cleitos thanked him solemnly. "I am the son of Conon," he explained.

"I thought as much. There is a likeness." As he said it, the young man looked unashamedly at Ala, who did indeed resemble her father. "I am Nicolaos, son of Nicander," he added.

Cleitos felt relieved. He knew Nicander at least by sight, and the acquaintance was a respectable one. He made no more objections as Eunice was hoisted groaning onto the back of his horse. Lydios took its bridle, and the farm boy followed with the mule, onto whose back he had managed to load Aletheia's chest tied on by the traces. The three young people walked quietly together, Cleitos carefully placing himself between Nicolaos and his sister.

Ala was not a bit shy. Eunice was in too much pain to fuss, and she felt her father would have made little of this accident. It was pleasant to listen while Nicolaos explained about the olive groves and the pottery they made because the clay was good in these parts. His father had bought a painter from a good workshop so that their best oil might be sold in costly jars. A coaster down at Brauron carried it around to Piraeus, whence it was shipped out on a merchantman. Since the family wealth came from this trade, his father liked to spend a part of the summer on his land. It happened, however, that this was his year for captaining a warship, so that Nicolaos had come in his stead to stay until harvest. "My military service is over," he explained.

Ala listened eagerly without perceiving that the conversation was intended to please her as much as her brother. Nicolaos, who had no sisters of his own, was curious about girls because his father thought he should soon marry. He was not sure he liked the idea, but when Ala peeped around her brother to see if he was still smiling, he caught her eye.

No notion of this kind entered Ala's head. She was only thinking how interesting men's conversation was and how much her brother already knew about oil and pots and trade. She was hoping that the farmer's wife would know what to do for Eunice, and she was secretly making up her mind to stay for the night. If trade was a man's affair, sickness was a woman's; and Ala already knew that she was just as responsible for Eunice as the elder woman was for her. A mistress must look out for her slaves, Athenais taught.

"If you wish to stay with us," said Nicolaos to Cleitos, "you need not fear to put us out. There are servants, and our women's court is large."

He had echoed Ala's thoughts exactly and, before she had time to remember that the young man was a perfect stranger, she answered impulsively, "I shall stay with Eunice until she is better."

Cleitos flushed to the roots of his hair, afraid to quell his sister, lest she start an argument. Nicolaos only laughed.

"You shall stay as long as you please," he said, looking at her directly. He grinned. "And your pretty bird also."

The
Temple

––––––––––

ALA STOOD BY HERSELF and looked around. The
priestess who had shown her into the room had left
her, saying that the girls were busy with their duties,
but that presently one would come to fetch her.
Perhaps she thought Ala needed time to cry a little;
but Ala felt more like smiling when she thought how
Nicolaos had caught her eye when she was told to
say good-bye to her two brothers. Cleitos had been
the one to be embarrassed. Nicolaos was taking him
on a visit to the headquarters of a nearby cavalry
troop. In his eagerness to meet his future com-
panions, Cleitos had persuaded himself that it did
not matter if Nicolaos rode with them to the temple, more especially as the farmer's wife sat with Ala
in the cart.

The mistake of the priestess had made an awk-
wardness. Farewells were hasty, and Nicolaos had
merely assured Ala again that the horse litter which
was carrying Eunice home would not jolt her. But
before Cleitos could stop him, he had bent for-

ward, winking an eye at the priestess and whispering to Ala, "She looks like a horse!" She did, with
a long mournful face, buck teeth, and hollow tem-
ples. It had been all that Ala could do not to giggle
on the spot.

Well, they were gone, and it was too late for tears. Besides, Ala was afraid she might be teased if her eyes were red. She looked around for something to do and straightened her chest beside the others. She wondered whether she might let Solon out of his cage, but she did not quite like to. He might, for one thing, make a mess; and the room was so clean.

Carefully she sat down on the bed, which rested on a framework of white stone built into the floor. It was laced with leather straps, on which lay a mattress smelling pleasantly of dried rushes. Ala put Solon's cage on her lap and folded her hands on top of it. There were eleven beds around the walls, all Ala's size, and with tables beside them. There was a row of chests with hers at one end, pegs on the wall with various things hanging from them, and a niche in which stood a small clay lamp. There was a basin on a stand and a jar beside it. Ala felt thirsty, but when she went over to look, the jar was empty.

There were no windows in the white room, but the wide doorway gave onto a courtyard, one side belonging to the temple and the opposite one to a colonnade. In the courtyard stood a splendid tree, in the shade of which lay signs of work: stools, a half-finished rush basket, wool, and spindles. Ala picked up Solon again and went quietly out.

Nobody was to be seen, but at least the court looked lived in. She found the water jars in a shaded corner sunk in the ground but with a small pitcher beside them for dipping out. Nearby stood a hand mill for grinding flour, pots and jars, a brazier for cooking, and a storage room curtained by onions plaited into strings with rushes.

She retreated, nervous of being caught prying, and went back. When she entered the little room, it took her a moment to see that she was in the wrong one. There were the same eleven beds, the tables and chests, but none was hers. For a second she was wild with fright; but she tiptoed out again, found her own bed next door, and sat on it, heart thumping.

Still nobody came. As she had entered the courtyard with the priestess, she had noticed how at the ends of the colonnade there lay the entrances to another one which seemed to lie behind the building. Cautiously she went out to explore. There was no one in the narrow colonnade behind the court which seemed to be devoted to votive offerings of various sorts, including women's garments. Ala went down the length of it to be sure it was quite empty.

She came back through the other entrance to the court, peeping cautiously along the colonnade as she rounded the corner. She gave a startled little jump. In it stood a girl with a rabbit in her arms, staring straight at her.

Ala went a frightened scarlet. "Oh! I was just looking for someone. I . . ." She put her hand to her mouth and stopped. Turning into the dim colonnade, she had not seen clearly for a moment. The little girl was marble. Someone giggled.

Ala swung around. In a doorway just beside her stood another little girl with another rabbit, only this time her hair was a reddish brown, her eyes were very blue, and the rabbit was a brown one with pink insides to his ears. He twitched his whiskers at her.

"You did, you did!" cried the little girl with a crow of triumph. "You spoke to the statue! I knew you would!"

Ala blushed deeply. She was not used to being laughed at, but there was one thing she could do. Hastily she set Solon on the ground and put her fingers into the corners of her eyes and nose and

mouth. She stretched them sideways and put her tongue out, having practiced the gesture privately at home.

"I saw you at the bear dance," she said when she relaxed.

The other girl nodded. "You are Aletheia, daughter of Conon, and I am Agarista, daughter of Eudoxos. Your father is an Olympic victor, and your mother is strict. My father is very rich indeed, and my mother is a beauty."

"Oh," said Ala, uncertain how to handle this information.

"Eudoxos saw my mother when she was carrying a basket of flowers in the procession of Athene, and he made his father ask for her. It was a good match."

"My mother made the robe for Athene," said Ala proudly.

Agarista took no notice. "I shall make a good match, too," she announced. "I am not so pretty, but then I shall have a much bigger dowry."

Already this was not the kind of conversation that Ala understood. She retreated onto safer ground. "May I stroke your rabbit? What is his name?"

"It's Hercules," Agarista said. She lowered her

voice. "I call him Whiskers! Look how he twitches them."

He did indeed twitch his whiskers, but Aletheia felt another shock. A name was something which belonged to a creature; and if you changed it, you might as well cut off its pink nose and offer it another. She stroked Hercules's soft fur, and he flattened his ears.

"Is that your bird? Why don't you take him out? Theodora has a dove, but she danced last year and will go home soon. Myro and Melinno have rabbits, but much smaller than Whiskers. I don't like Myro and Melinno much. They go about with their arms around each other and talk secrets. They call themselves the M's. Let's be the A's!"

This time Ala knew exactly what she wanted to answer. "Oh, do let's!"

A single moon season had hardly gone by before the house of Conon had faded in Ala's mind to a far-off place, beloved it is true, but so different from the temple that it might as well have belonged to another girl. How hopeless, for instance, to imagine that earlier Ala collecting spiders to put in the beds of Myro and Melinno, or rolling on her bed, stifling giggles until Melinno screamed.

"Why didn't Myro notice?" she wondered next morning. "Do you think she rolled over and squashed them?"

Agarista shook her head. "No, she didn't. I looked."

"What are you two whispering about?" asked Myro crossly.

Ala and Agarista looked at each other. "Secrets!" They giggled.

The priestess set in charge of the girls was a dreamy woman who seldom noticed what they did as long as their sacred duties were performed. If Ala and Agarista were sent out to gather flowers for the shrine, she did not worry if they dawdled. She was only careful to see they took a flint knife, since nothing cut by metal must ever be brought into the shrine of the goddess. As long as they were quiet in the temple, she did not mind if they ran shrieking through the courtyard. If they learned the ancient prayers but left their spinning tasks half done, it did not matter.

She had little trouble with them when it came to their real duties. The girls swept out the shrine, washed the sacred vessels, laid sticks on the altar for little fires which consumed scatterings of meal or drops of wine and oil. They kept the dormitories

clean, both their own and those which were reserved for pilgrims. They recited some of the prayers and attended the chief priestess, standing beside her with the day's offerings in their hands.
They sang hymns to the goddess, some of which
were so old and strange that their magic phrases had
to be explained by the priestess.

The service of the temple was always solemn,
for the girls were in awe of the image. From the
moment she saw it, Ala felt as though she was looking into a deep, cold well, from the very bottom of
which something unseen stared back.

The image was wooden and black, glistening
with oil even in the semidarkness of its cool shrine.
It was shaped like a tree trunk; and on the front
of it was carved an oblong face, smooth and hair-
less, with eyes inset by two red stones, a long, narrow nose, immense upper lip, and thin mouth set
in a tight smile. Below the face, a tiny body was
shown only by fine lines in the rounded wood, its
little arms crossed over the breasts and little legs
drawn up against the stomach as if the goddess
were in a squatting position.

When Ala came in to sweep or sprinkle cool water on the floor, she would look at the image and it
would stare at her with a small, cruel smile. Ala's

skin would prickle, perhaps with the coolness of the dim shrine, or perhaps because the goddess was still thinking of those distant, bloody days when Iphigenia was her priestess.

The presence of the image lay like a small, dark shadow on the temple; but the actual worship of moon goddess Artemis was beautiful and touching. It went on in simple offerings and prayers of country people, and in queer old rituals or chants. In either case it went on in the heart of the priestess. This, the older priestesses taught, was a Mystery, something that grew up between a priestess and her god. It was not to be understood, but to be felt; for in this way the gods were known by men.

The bear dance was part of this Mystery. Every moon they learned a little of it and danced for the goddess in the court before the temple. Each step made a special pattern, with its own meaning, so that by dancing one could talk with Artemis. Yet it was not through the figure each made by herself, but all together that they spoke with the goddess and received answer in no language.

Solon was part of the Mystery, too. Every girl had her own pet, a squirrel or a starling, a rabbit or a dove. It seemed that the goddess spoke more freely with animals than with men. Thus Solon,

who went almost everywhere with Ala, would cock
his head at strange moments, fly into a tree and sit
cooing. Then he was talking with the goddess, but
at other moments he spoke in Ala's ear as he sat on
her shoulder. It was as if something in the bird
brought god and man together.

Perhaps the center of the Mystery was understood by the country people. At certain times of
the moon they came to the temple with simple offerings, not all together in procession, but just when
they needed the goddess. A peasant might bring
his donkey and his wife, both big with child, to ask
that Artemis might grant them both a safe delivery.
Because he wanted to make sure that the goddess
knew him from others in like case, he mumbled to
her about the troubles they had had the last time
and what they hoped for. Women who had lost
their earlier children poured out their laments.
Later on, they would bring their babies, if things
had gone well, to give thanks to the goddess.

So many children had been lost, so many pains
suffered! So many women prayed in vain that the
goddess would grant them a healthy son! Sometimes with tears in her eyes Ala wondered at the
cruelty of the goddess. Yet when a woman came
back with her child, she had no memory of the past,

except that her joy was all the greater for it. She spoke to Artemis as to a dear friend who had helped her out of trouble.

About the end of the second moon, Lydios rode over on a donkey to leave a bundle with the priestesses for Ala. It contained a second blanket for the nights, which were getting colder, a pretty box inlaid with a picture of a dancing bear in ivory, another set of ribbons from poor Phyllis, a batch of Eunice's honey cakes, and a letter. It said,

Conon is gone to consult the god at Delphi. He has taken Cleitos with him. Eunice walks with a staff, but she is well. Phyllis has broken the big bowl with the satyr pictures. Remember all women love best things they have suffered for. Callina writes this. Farewell.

It was a beautiful letter. Ala read it over and over, especially the part that Athenais had bid her remember. She even showed it in a serious moment to Agarista, who opened her blue eyes very wide. "You mean you can *read* it?"

"Callina taught me," Ala said. "My mother wished it."

Agarista bit into a honey cake. "*My* mother,"

she retorted, "says it is not good for a woman to learn things reserved for men."

"Well, what *does* your mother do?" asked Ala crossly. She had already discovered that Agarista's mother did not like weaving and spinning because they ruined the hands.

"She makes medicines," said Agarista unexpectedly, "out of herbs and spells and things. She makes beauty washes, too. Once she made a love potion, and she told me not to drink it, but I did."

"What happened?" Ala's mouth hung open in horror.

"Nothing. It tasted horrible, and I threw up."

"Oh!"

"I expect I should have fallen in love with Manon," said Agarista grandly. "He's very good-looking."

"Who's Manon?" As Ala could not remember having met anyone to fall in love with, she was impressed.

"My father's boy. He plays the flute at parties and dances sometimes, too."

"Not a *slave!*" Ala was deeply shocked.

Agarista smiled knowingly. "Why not? It would have been practice." She tried to look as though she had a vast experience. "It keeps one's hand in." She giggled.

"Oh!" said Ala solemnly, taking this in.

Agarista helped herself to another cake and munched, dismissing the subject.

Fall came and winter came. Rain turned the courtyard into a sea of mud so that everything in it had to be huddled under cover. The girls wore their cloaks all day and warmed nipped fingers and toes at a tiny brazier. Solon crouched in his cage and looked unhappy. He did not like the mud which was everywhere.

When the priestess said the dawn prayer at Artemis's altar, her breath went up like smoke; and the chanting was long and tedious and cold. There was no bear dance at the full of the moon because the goddess was hidden by dark clouds, and it was raining. Even the country folk came seldom through the dirty roads because it was not easy in this season to spare a gift for the goddess from the storehouse.

The nose of the buck-toothed priestess was red, and a drop hung from the end of it. Eunice's medicine was coming in useful.

"It ought to do you good," said Ala anxiously. "It tastes so bitter."

Agarista nodded. "But my throat's still sore."

"It might feel worse if you hadn't had any."

"It might feel better, too," said Agarista with spirit. "I don't think I'll drink any more, and we'll see if I'm better or worse."

"All right."

"I wish I were home."

Ala made no answer to this, except to put her head in her hands and burst into tears. But when Agarista asked her if she wanted to go home, too, she shook her head. "I thought of something I didn't want to . . . think about . . . just yet." She sobbed again.

Spring came with sunshine and flowers. The girls had new masks for the bear dance, and they danced it with twinkling feet, outstripping the pipes. There were new hymns to be sung for the goddess as shepherds came up with the firstlings of their flocks, the young spring lambs. There was blood instead of wine and oil on the altar; but the fire consumed it all in thick, dark smoke. The shepherds went home whistling, and part of the meat was left for the temple.

"I don't like the killing," Ala said to Agarista.

Agarista shrugged. "Nobody does, but how else would anyone eat?"

"The high priestess does. I watched her."

"Oh, the priestess! She has to, of course."

The red anemones were out in the fields. Agarista was wild to try some magic. There was magic all around them in the temple, in the ancient words they said before the goddess, in the high crown worn by the priestess, which was of gold and once had belonged to Iphigenia. There was queer magic in a painted bird, which sat on a pedestal in the temple and which, if you turned a wheel, would re-

volve and sing. But magic art of this kind was too lofty for one's own ends. It merely whetted the appetite for simple spells. All the girls had collections of luck-stones and bits of snakeskin, eagle feathers, and dried roots cut with stone knives at the full of the moon. Country women gave cakes for these treasures, and it was prudent to keep one or two for oneself in case of need.

They learned good-luck words it was wise to say on waking, and watched good-luck birds flying past them on the right. All the girls knew love spells, some rather crude, which peasant women had imparted to the maids of Artemis. Someone had told Agarista that on the days when dark and light are equal a maid might stand at dawn under the boughs of a hawthorn with one foot on land and one in water, with a living thing in her arms and a dead thing on her head. Then she must say a secret spell and look in the water, where she would see the face of the man she was going to marry.

"There's a hawthorn across the river," she said, "by the stone where we wash our clothes. I know there is."

"It's outside the temple grounds," objected Ala. "And every girl in Brauron will be there too."

"They won't," said Agarista triumphantly. "The

words are very secret, and I had to give my green beads to learn them." Agarista's green beads were of carved jade from Egypt, very costly and an object of envy to all the girls in the temple. She tossed her head with a careless air. "My father will give me more when I am married," said she.

It was only because of the green beads that Ala consented. This magic was something that she did not want any part in for secret reasons of her own. It belonged to the thought that she tried not to think, not till after the bear dance. But now it lay between her and Agarista, even while they giggled and plotted how to sneak out, so that, just as if she had a sore tooth that she could not help exploring with her tongue, she found herself saying, "Why do you want to get married, Agarista?"

Agarista looked startled. "Every girl does, and I'm nearly fourteen."

"But will you like it?"

Agarista was sure she would. "I shall laugh a lot and wear pretty things; and my mother will give me my old nurse to go with me and be my house-keeper. I shall have babies as the peasant women do, only mine will be nicer. I expect I shall like my husband because my father is very wise and kind, but of course I want to know whom he will choose. Don't you?"

Ala went a bright scarlet. "I don't know."

Agarista opened her blue eyes wide and stared at Ala. "You mean, you don't want to get married at all?"

"Stupid!" snapped Ala crossly. "Of course I do."

Agarista decided that Ala was frightened lest witch wife Hecate send something ugly to look over her shoulder which she would have to marry afterwards. But Ala said it was no such thing, but would Agarista take her turn at sweeping out the house of the goddess. She did not say why.

Actually, when the time came, both girls were frightened. It was really wicked to stray outside the temple grounds, while the river, still running high in spring, was bitter cold. Ala had Solon in her hands and Callina's beads in her hair. She was shivering, and Solon seemed uneasy, too. He tried to flutter away. "Be quick," she whispered. "Somebody might see us." In the growing light their white robes would show up. There was no telling what might be done to them for leaving the temple.

Agarista began to say the words. Witch goddess Hecate, half nightmare and half woman, was a

make out her own white robe and Ala's by it. Surely those were branches of the tree, or were they eddies? She bent closer . . . Surely . . .

Clear on the wind came the whistle of a shepherd coming up the pasture, breaking into a gay tune.

"Quick, quick! He'll find us!" Both in panic fled to the stepping stones that crossed the river. It was not till they were safe in the temple precinct, wet and panting, that Agarista said:

"I saw something. I really did, only it wasn't clear. If that man hadn't come! Did you see anything, Ala?"

The things that Ala would not think about had been shaken to the surface. She said, teeth chattering, "I s-saw what I expected to see, just me and S-Solon. You see, I'm not going to get married, ever."

Agarista stared at her, struck absolutely dumb.

"R-remember when Theodora went home," Ala said. "She had a bird like me. She gave it to Artemis, and the priestess . . ." She choked on the words. "Would you let her kill Whiskers over the altar?"

Agarista bent over Whiskers and kissed his fur. "But you know I have to! Whiskers is me. He's my . . . he's my maidenhood to give to the goddess. When Iphigenia was snatched away from the altar, there was a fawn instead. There has to be something always. You know that there has to." She buried her nose in Whiskers's fur and breathed deeply of his rabbit smell. "We belong to Artemis, and something of us has to stay with her for the rest of our lives. It's part of the Mystery."

"I know," Ala said, white but determined. "I did not want to think about it until after the bear dance in case I felt different by then. But I know now that I can't give Solon, and so I shall have to stay with Artemis myself. I'm not going home."

The
Mystery

EVERY DAY Aletheia looked in the polished mirror
which her mother had given her, because Agarista
said that if she stayed in the temple, she would grow
like the other priestesses. There was the buck-
toothed one with the silly expression, the one with
a mole and black hairs on her lip who taught them
the bear dance, the pockmarked one, the one that
squinted, and the sallow high priestess with the long
nose and tight smile like that of the image.

"I couldn't be like them all," protested Ala.

"You'll see," said Agarista threateningly.

Aletheia did see that her face had grown longer
and her cheekbones were beginning to stick out.
Her nose had changed, too, and her chin was bonier
than it ever used to be. She pretended she did not
mind, but she stared in the mirror so often that the
girls began to tease her.

"Aletheia's got a lover!" chanted Melinno.

"You leave Ala alone, or I'll hit you," flashed
Agarista.

"Don't you dare hurt Melinno!" Myro cried.

Tempers were touchy just now; but before the quarrel flared into blows, Philodamia put in a head to say that some great lady was arriving at the temple. This was so unusual a sight at this season, owing to the distance from Athens and the badness of spring roads for wheeled traffic, that everyone went out to have a look.

The lady talking to the buck-toothed priestess was neither young nor, as it appeared, in any trouble. Indeed, she was so comfortable looking with her short, stout figure and pleasant smile that she might easily have passed for somebody's old nurse, were it not for the richness of her cloak and the gold pins in her hair. The buck-toothed priestess beckoned Aletheia and Agarista to attend at the offering of the presents which servants were taking from the cart.

The stout lady beamed on them both. "Now which is Agarista? Ah, now I see you have a look which tells me that you are daughter of a famous beauty! So this is Aletheia, then. My son, Nicolaos, spoke of your kindness to your nurse and how long you stayed with her until she was better."

She patted Ala, taking no notice of the fact that she had gone beet red. "You must know that my name is Artemidora; and a long time ago when I was young and slim, I danced the bear dance and slept in one of your little beds behind the temple. You would not think it to look at me now; but when I left, my father gave a statue of me as I was then. It stands somewhere or other."

"Oh, now I know," cried Ala eagerly. "You are the little girl with the rabbit at the entrance of the colonnade. It says Artemidora, daughter of Philemon, gave it."

"So you can read!" said Artemidora thoughtfully. "Unusual!" She seemed to ponder. "But I like it. We women have all too little in our heads." She smiled again at them both and said, "When the sacrifice is over, you shall show me the statue, for it was put up after I left and I never saw it. Perhaps you will show me the little beds, too, and the old courtyard. And then you must take me into the shrine to pay my respects to the image."

She turned to accompany the priestess; and as the girls followed after, Agarista whispered in Ala's ear. "Who's her son Nicolaos? How can he know who you are?"

"It was an accident," Ala whispered back. "He helped us when Eunice was hurt."

This sounded more romantic than anything that

had happened to Agarista. She murmured furiously, "Why didn't you tell me all about it?"

Ala felt surprised herself. She said, wondering, "I simply forgot it."

Artemidora was delighted with the statue. "It's not very like me; but then they are not meant to be, you know. My mouth was really too wide to please the goddess." She wanted to see the beds and said she had slept in Melinno's, but that she was afraid it would not bear her now. Perhaps if she sat on the very edge they might get her a drink of water from the court. It was cooler out of the sun.

They gave her a drink and she gave them some almond cakes which she hoped were better than the ones the country people paid for luck charms. She smiled at them as she said it, and they smiled too because this traffic was carried on behind the backs of the elder priestesses. Presently they were talking as though they were all girls together. Artemidora had danced one of the solos in the bear dance, the one where the spirit is frightened and runs away. Aletheia was trying the joyful one at the end, but she found it difficult. The leaps were so hard.

"The joyful one is the worst of all," agreed Artemidora. She looked keenly at Ala. "Especially

since it comes near the end, where the dancing is
harder. The end is a difficult time."

Ala nodded, but she did not say anything.
Agarista was dancing the funny one where the bears
of the woodland are beginning to feel the powers
of the goddess. She got up and showed what she

was doing, while Artemidora laughed and gave her hints.

Time passed so pleasantly that it slipped by unnoticed. Artemidora looked out into the court and gave a sharp cry. "Look how the shadows have moved while we sat talking! The priestess will be angry with me for keeping you from your duties. Indeed, I think that Agarista had better go and explain that Aletheia must take me into the temple to visit the goddess."

It was cool and quiet in the house of the goddess. The red-eyed image stared as it always did, and Aletheia shivered.

"Do you never look at the image?" Artemidora said, speaking quietly, as was fitting in the house of the goddess. "You must come with me this way, and I will show you a thing."

She drew Aletheia far to one side. Here one saw only the high forehead, the long nose, and the deep line running down the edge of the smooth cheek, past the corner of the tiny mouth above the pointed chin. Looked at this way, there was a still sadness about the goddess as she bowed her head forward over the hands on her breasts, too small to help. "She listens to many troubles," said Artemidora, "but as you see, she feels."

Aletheia said nothing, but stared for a moment at the goddess. Then she turned and flung her arms around Artemidora, clinging to her as though she were Athenais after something had gone wrong in the women's court.

Artemidora patted her. "There, there! I knew you were in trouble when I first set eyes on you. I well remember . . . but never mind that now. Your mother never danced the bear dance, did she? She was maid of Athene. If she had known our Mystery, she might have taught you to be less wise and more lighthearted. Nicolaos said you were too kind."

Aletheia said, her voice muffled by Artemidora's shoulder, "I'm not kind! I'm not! Sometimes I hate the bird."

"Then can you not give it up?"

Aletheia shook her head, and when she was asked about her reason, she shook it again. Too many miseries had pressed upon her at once, and all was in confusion. Artemidora was forced to give up questioning her. "I'm a plain, ignorant old woman," she said heaving a sigh, "and my Mystery will be different from yours. Each has her own. I have no daughters either, but I will tell you what I know. One moment our girls are children, playing that dolls are people. Sometimes hardly a year goes by before they are married and find how sorrow and pain come mixed with joy. You have heard how the women pour out their troubles before the goddess. How can we bear what they bear if we have not a Mystery in our hearts, giving knowledge of sorrow? This is the meaning of the Mystery, except that for some it is harder than for others."

"Then Agarista has her Mystery, too."

"Even though she likes to laugh? Yes, Agarista has it, but she will not speak of it, I daresay. You must not press her."

Aletheia felt comforted. In the days that followed, she laughed with Agarista again as she told her about the adventure when she had met Nicolaos. "I only stayed because Eunice was in such pain, and I did not think of much else. Except that manners were not so formal in the country, and the farmer's wife was jolly. Nicolaos came in and out of the court as though he had been her own son."

Agarista thought herself too old to giggle, but she opened her eyes wide in surprise. After that, she often made jokes about Nicolaos. Between the two girls, friendship was stronger than ever, except that they never spoke about the Mystery. In thoughtful moments Aletheia liked to go into the temple now that she knew the goddess understood what was in her heart. Perhaps Artemis might find a way at the bear dance, which was a time when the goddess spoke to her maidens. If not, Artemidora had said something at parting.

"When I was a girl," said Artemidora vaguely, "things used to go on which were not talked about, and they never did any harm. Or I don't think so . . . Well, if your Mystery is too hard for you, send me a token. Send me your pretty beads, perhaps. Any country woman will carry them because we are well known in these parts. Three days later, go across the stepping stones and wait under the hawthorn until the sun comes up." She smiled at Ala. "You know, I always pretend I never met my husband until my bridal day, but it is not quite true!"

Ala looked at her, startled and questioning.

"You must not mind how I run on," said Artemidora. "Only do not be frightened under your hawthorn. Other couples have used that place before because it is outside the temple."

Artemidora had said no more because her cart was waiting. Now morning and evening and whenever she opened her chest, Ala felt for the beads.

Another thing that helped came five days later,

long enough, had Ala thought, for a message from
Artemidora to be received and digested in Athens.
It was a bundle containing another set of ribbons
from Phyllis, a tonic from Eunice, Callina's precious luck-stone wrapped in a fragment of gold tis-
sue, and a set of pretty gold brooches to fasten the
sleeves of the bear costume. With these came another letter:

Nicander came to visit Conon. Cleitos has joined the cavalry. Eunice says spring medicine is good for the blood. Phyllis is learning to embroider. Callina wishes you better luck than she had. Remember, growing is pain as well as pleasure. Farewell.

"Nicander has asked for you for Nicolaos!" exclaimed Agarista at once. She sighed. "Oh, how I wish someone would ask my father for me!"

"What nonsense!" Aletheia said. "I don't believe it." But in her heart she did believe it, and the thought gave far more comfort than the maxims of Athenais. If Nicander had truly asked for her, then the future was settled, and the Mystery would have to work itself out. Perhaps the goddess would release her by taking the bird to herself. Perhaps . . . Aletheia brooded; and she woke the dormitory a few days later by calling loudly in her sleep for Nicolaos.

"Sh! He's her brother!" Agarista hissed. "Don't wake her!"

"But her brother's Cleitos," said Melinno sharply.

"The one that died," lied Agarista desperately.

Dead silence fell in the dormitory. To be visited by the ghost of someone dead must mean a summons. Even to hear his name could be unlucky. All the girls stopped their ears, and none of them said a word to Aletheia. They merely watched her, heads together, as she practiced the leaps of the bear dance. Hope was springing up in her heart and she soared lightly, while the priestess said she had always known that Ala could do it.

Dance
on the
Mountains!

THE HIGH PRIESTESS left the temple in a procession
several days before the bear dance, dressed in the
stately robes of Iphigenia. Men carried her in a
booth set on poles, and everyone came out to see
her pass. In the villages, the little girls wore crude
bear masks of leather and ran shrieking hand in
hand through the streets. If they could encircle a
man, he must pay forfeit in sweetmeats made of
chopped nuts and honey no bigger than a thumb-
nail. Grandfathers, who were easiest to catch, paid
generously, stuffing small mouths with things to
chew or suck. Workworn mothers looked smiling
on, some spinning, others with baskets of sweets to
ransom their men when they were captured.

At night there was dancing in the marketplace,
nothing rehearsed for the goddess, but simply the
old traditional steps that all men knew. If there was
a rich man in the place, he gave a great bowl of
wine which, mixed with water, stood by as a re-

freshment for the dancers. There were no sacrifices in these villages, except for the pouring of wine and oil on a rough altar of beaten earth and the burning of pine logs. The booth was wreathed with fresh flowers night and morning, and relays of bearers took it on to the next stage of its journey.

They rested for the last night not far from the gates of Athens. Next morning the elders of the city came out to meet them, escorted by young boys dressed in white. These were the children whose mothers had died in giving them birth and who for that reason were under special protection of the goddess. The little priestesses rode through the streets in carts drawn by white oxen, alighting to wind up the Acropolis in front of the high priest-ess, carrying branches of laurel. Behind her came the young boys singing a hymn, followed by men driving sheep and goats for the formal sacrifices.

Blood ran and wine was poured while the sun mounted in the heavens and turned westward. Rich, oily smoke rose into the sky; and meat was but-chered for the public feast in the town hall which honored the goddess. With all these ceremonies the little priestesses had nothing to do. This was the occasion for Iphigenia herself, as it had been of old in Tauris.

The dancers gathered behind the booth in a small place screened with laurel as the sun dipped close to the hills on the western horizon. They were washed and rubbed with fine oils, they were scented with perfume; and their yellow dresses were new for the occasion. They had their bear masks on because these were fastened by straps beneath their clothes, lest they shift with the dancing. Agarista was a round and laughing bear for the funny scene, while Aletheia was a tall black one for the final solo. Presently they could hear the priestess begin her prayer. After she finished, the shrill flutes began to call up the moon.

It was all so familiar by now that they could have danced it without so much as thinking what it meant. But the holiness of the spot, the ring of torches, the girls and men looking on gave it fresh life. Every so often as they twisted and turned, they caught glimpses of Athene's temple, silver in the moonlight, or saw some little girl on her father's shoulders bend forward, clutching his hair.

These pictures came and went while steadily the feet beat out their patterns on the sand. They were not dancing for the goddess with their minds, but with their bodies, not each for herself, but all together, crying that life was beautiful and ugly,

strange and savage, and very old. The goddess watched in the sky, and the priestess in her booth.

Joy was hardest at the end because sweat was trickling into the eyes and the inside of the bear mask was wet with panting breath. Yet the spirit must lift itself in joy, just as the leaves come out in spring and the birds sing merrily, forgetting the cold. The effort of those soaring leaps was the striving of the spirit to burst free and rejoice. There was a stitch in Ala's side, and her breath came in harsh panting; but she danced for the goddess as the green leaves dance in the wind.

It was ending quietly, as it always did. The men began singing, "Goddess of Mothers, daughter of Leto, dance on the mountains . . ." and the little voices joined in, "Protectress of maidens . . . in your white temple . . . watch over our land." The dance was over, and the girls had spoken with their goddess about a Mystery which belonged, not to each one, but to all mankind.

They did not think it over at the time. They were very tired; the place was strange, and the hour late. Next day there would be more sacrifices for the priestess, who did not set out on her leisurely way back until the day after. The little dancers had played their part and might spend one day at home.

The women's court in the house of Conon was dearer and smaller and dustier. There were a few gray hairs in Athenais's head, and Eunice was very lame. When Conon kissed his daughter, he said, "Another thing well done! I said good-bye to a little girl, and now I find a pretty maiden . . . if only she were not so thin."

Ala blushed and laughed, but she was shy with Conon, lest he talk to her about Nicolaos before she was ready.

There was a new girl in the women's court, a red-cheeked barbarian from the north who spoke bad Greek and already adored Athenais. "Phyllis waits a good deal on Eunice, and then I like a girl to train," explained Athenais. She smiled lovingly at Ala. "Besides, we shall need trained servants for you before long."

Nothing more could be said because, though she and Athenais sat together, Eunice was close to them, while the red-cheeked handmaid hovered with something to show or a question for Athenais.

It was a happy day, yet if the goddess had found an answer for Ala, the house of Conon had no idea of it. Once when Eunice had been helped up to look at the cooking, Athenais said, "Your father would like you home very soon. After all, you are nearly grown up; and there is the future to consider."

Ala felt frightened at once. She answered quickly, "There are still duties which I am meant to perform. It is not yet a year."

Athenais squeezed her fondly. "If it must be so . . . but, Aletheia . . ." This time it was Callina who came up with her stool and her spinning.

When the priestess set off with them to return to the temple, Agarista was brimming with excitement. "Phylarchos has offered his son! Think of it! Phylarchos, whose chariot won at the Delphic games last year! My mother says the boy is so good-looking!"

"How does she know?"

Agarista's eyes twinkled. "My father brought in a famous artist to have the labors of Hercules painted on the walls of his banquet hall. So my mother had the servants bore a hole through the eye of Hercules, so that she could stand on a stool and look through the wall when she wanted."

Aletheia laughed. She had long ago given up being shocked by Agarista. "What would your father do if he found out?"

"Oh, I expect he would tease her about some of the stories men like to tell when they are alone together. He always laughs at what my mother does."

Agarista thought she would have to go home soon. Her mother said Phylarchos was eager to arrange the affair, and she by now was turned fourteen. She considered a moment, looking at Ala.

"I'll stay as long as I can," she promised. Aletheia squeezed her hand.

When they got back to the temple, Solon was glad to see his mistress. He flew up onto her shoulder; but as she stroked him, she thought how she had hoped the goddess would take him while she was away. Solon spread his pretty tail and cooed as sweetly as ever, while the image stood with her folded hands in the temple, and everything else went on just as before.

In another moon a message was sent to Agarista that her father was coming to fetch her in ten days. She went perfectly white, and Ala discovered her a few hours later down by the hutch where Whiskers lived, feeding him dandelion leaves and crying.

"He's only a rabbit," she said defiantly.

"I know he is," agreed Ala. "Never mind."

Agarista dashed away tears with the back of her hand. "I shan't ever see you, except at the theater perhaps once a year, or the feast of Athene . . . If

you wrote letters, I might get somebody to read them and write you an answer . . . But letters don't say much."

"They don't, do they?"

"My father's giving a statue of me, and I daresay yours is, too. They might stand together."

"I should like that."

Agarista brightened up. "I shall twist my husband around my finger," she announced firmly, "and make him let me pay visits. Some women do."

Aletheia smiled a little. "I daresay you will."

Agarista turned to her rabbit again, and Aletheia perceived it was one of those moments when animals speak to the heart more deeply than men. She took Solon in her two hands and went out into the meadow. There she threw him up into the air, but he would only circle and try to alight again upon her shoulder. She picked up a branch and beat him away. "Go on," she said. "Fly free! I let your wings grow for the purpose."

The bird flew up into a tree and sat there waiting. "Go away," cried Ala clapping her hands. She picked up a stone to scare him off.

A hawk came flapping with lazy speed across the river, and Aletheia watched it circle, looking for prey. It caught sight of something on the other side of the copse and darted after it. Solon flew back to Ala's shoulder, and she had to let him stay.

She went back with dragging feet toward the temple, brooding over what was in her heart. Even Agarista took it for granted that Ala's future was settled and that in a month or two she would give Solon to the goddess and go home. She herself did not want to renounce her life for a temple which was white and cold without Agarista, or for an image which pitied but did not help. Soon a message would come to her from her father, and what could she do then? Conon was not a tyrant, but he expected to be obeyed. She felt sick at the thought of his anger, even though she knew he would not force her away. It had been Conon himself who had said of her gift, "Not till you choose."

Everything but one had failed her. Agarista was going. The goddess was silent. Athenais, maid of Athene, loved without understanding. No one was left but Artemidora to help her. Aletheia went to her chest and took out the beads which Callina had painted. Artemidora had said that certain things went on which were not talked of, and Aletheia knew quite well what they were. She was ashamed to send because of what she thought; but now she saw no help for it.

Any country woman, Artemidora had said, would take the token. Aletheia went out to find one with a kind face who understood trouble.

The
Bird in
the Hand

THE LIGHT WAS GROWING GRAY when Aletheia
crossed the river to meet with Nicolaos under the
hawthorn. She came shyly, still a little ashamed of
having sent for him; but he only smiled at her with
his kind look, saying, "I sent my mother to see if
she could like you, and now she has sent me . . .
Pretty bird!"

He put out a hand to ruffle Solon's feathers, but
the bird stepped onto it and sidled down his arm.
He began to stroke it with the tip of his other fore-
finger, letting Ala get used to his presence, just as if
she were the bird.

"What shall we do with the pretty bird?" he
asked quietly. "Shall we let him go free?"

"I tried, but he would not fly away. Then a hawk
came over."

Nicolaos nodded. "I do not think he would live
long by himself. He is too tame."

"I made him tame," said Aletheia in a tight, angry voice.

"He was your bird."

She shook her head. "I did not have to make him trust me and sing for me and take a seed for me, since all the time I knew what was intended. This fate was none of his choosing, for he loves life as much as I."

Nicolaos put out his hand and took hers. "Sit down on this old stump and look at the river while I sit at your feet. See how slowly the current moves at this season, and yet it goes to the sea. Will it help you if I say that no one chooses fate? We are neither born when we wish, nor die when we desire. The bird, too, has its fate; and part of this is surely that while it lived it was fated to be happy. People say that we should not lament such fortune, since those whom the gods love best die young."

Aletheia reflected, looking at the river going by without a ripple. Behind her in the thickets, the sparrows began to pipe up the sun. Presently she explained, "When the high gods make a pet of a child, they do not give him to death themselves. The god of the underworld comes when it is fated. I have been like the high gods to my bird, and now

you ask me to be god of death as well. I cannot do that."

"This is your fate," he said.

"I know, and yet I cannot."

"Aletheia," said Nicolaos, "let me tell you what a very wise man used to teach about death. He said that life and death were opposites and could not touch each other. There is life in every man and bird and beast, yet if it is truly life, how can death blow it out like a candle? Bodies die, but the life that is in them must find another body. Every instant things are being born as well as dying."

"You mean, my bird will become another bird?"

"Or beast, or even man. Who knows? But the happy spirit which you have loved in him lives on, like the rain which falls in winter and dries out of the land and falls again."

Aletheia looked Nicolaos in the eyes. "Do you believe this?"

"I do believe it," he said, "but I must warn you that other wise men say many different things."

Aletheia gave a long sigh. She seemed to relax, but she only asked, "Does your mother believe it?"

"Let us hope she believes it," he said gently, "since my two older brothers were both killed in the sea battle three years ago."